D0525462

COVE

C016295732

Cove

Cynan Jones

GRANTA

Granta Publications, 12 Addison Avenue, London W11 4QR

First published in Great Britain by Granta Books, 2016

The opening of this novel is a version of a microfiction piece,
'Lifeboat', published in *New Welsh Review 100*, summer 2013.

A CIP catalogue record for this book is available
from the British Library.

1 3 5 7 9 10 8 6 4 2

ISBN 978 1 84708 881 9
ISBN 978 1 84708 883 3

Typeset in Vendome by Lindsay Nash

Printed and bound by
CPI Group (UK) Ltd, Croydon, CR0 4YY

www.grantabooks.com

MIX
Paper from
responsible sources
FSC® C020471

For C.

Cove[1] (kəʊv) n. a small bay or inlet; a sheltered place.

Cove[2] (kəʊv) n. a fellow; a man.

You hear, on the slight breeze, the *tunt tunt, tunt tunt* before you see the boat. You feel illicit.

When the boat comes alongside they cut the engine. Shout.

Waves break, the breeze. You don't hear. Swash filters in the pools.

A man in the prow carries a boat hook as if it's a harpoon. They are in drysuits, white helmets, bright life jackets.

One of the crew seats himself on the gunwale and pushes himself into the water. He swims strangely, held up by the lifejacket, lifted and pushed by the water. Like a spaceman.

You are not sure whether the kick comes from the baby or the sureness he has news.

When he comes from the water he stumbles and trips on the stones, clearing his nose of seawater. As if re-finding himself.

For some reason he takes off his gloves as he talks.

'Have you been on the beach?' he asks.

You nod. Say, 'Yes.' You cannot hide the subtle bell of your stomach now. 'I was on the fields for a while but came down. Around the point.'

When he moves the water falls from inside his life-jacket. He seems to wait for it.

'There's a missing child,' he says.

The boat floats behind the man, prey, unpowered, to the shift and swell. You hear the engine crack, rattle off the high shale cliffs. The crew bring the boat round. Then cut the motor again.

The man's face is reddened, shocked-looking after the water.

You went down to the beach after finding the pigeon.

First the burst of feathers; further on, the wing, torn off at the shoulder. It had blown across the field like a sail, the sinews and scraps of it dried translucent in the sun.

The rest of the bird was by the stile.

The head was gone, the meat of its chest. The breastbone oddly, industriously clean.

Then you saw the rings. One blue, one red. The red slightly split. The blue one glassy and unnatural on the leg.

You had a strange sense of horror from the pigeon. That it knew before being struck. Of it trying to get home. Of something throwing it off course.

You feel you must return the rings. Let the person it belongs to know.

You pull the leg, try to break the joint. Pull more strongly until the limb rips from the socket.

A peregrine, you think. Try to snap the knee with the act of loosening wire.

In the end, you use a stone to crush the leg repeatedly until the rings slip off.

You go onto the beach to clean your hands.

The sand is wet, intimate. There is the faint sugary crunch, the smallest suction under your feet, the wash, the wish of the sea.

Turnstones rise and *peep* ahead, flashing for a moment before they drop a few yards on. And because you did so as a child, you go to the seaweed strewn at the high water line and turn it with your feet. Sandhoppers flick chaotically.

The water is cool on your hands, your bending awkward now. With your thumb you rub a toffee of dark blood away and it seems to unfurl in the salt water, thread out in the pool.

A little way off you see something you think is a wetsuit shoe and the world tips, until you realise it's a trainer, colourful, like a tiny shelduck.

When you stand, where you held your weight against a rock, the dents of barnacles are in your skin.

The man speaks into his radio, pinches the handset on his chest and speaks. You see the crew receive him, answer, hear the boat motor in the radio, as if you suddenly hear the man's organs, his heart.

'No. It's clear,' he says.

The wear of the slow search crosses his eyes. As if, for a split second, it is very early morning.

He puts his gloves back on and nods, steps back into the sea.

As he swims you see them dip the boat hook, pull something from the water. They examine it then throw it back and it bobs like a duck.

They help the man back in. You see him shake his head and point.

Then you watch them as they head out, in a line across the bay.

It's only when they've gone you realise they've missed something, there, at the edge of the tide.

When you get to it, it is a doll.

PART I

He is holding his hands in the water, rubbing the blood from them, when the hairs on his arms stand up. They sway briefly, like seaweed in the current. Then lie down again.

He looks up. A strange ruffle come across the surface.

The birds had lifted suddenly and gone away. As if there were some signal. They are flecks now, a hiatus disappearing against the light off the sea.

He is far enough out for the land to have paled in view.

The first lightning strikes out somewhere past the horizon. At first he thinks it some sudden glint. The thunder happens moments later, and he feels sick in his guts.

A metallic sheen comes to the water, like cutlery. Like metal much touched. The white clouds glow, go a sort of leaden at the edge.

There was a delay, he thinks. Enough delay. Sees the rain as a thick dark band, moving in. Starts to paddle.

Then there is a wire of electric brightness...Three. Four...A rumble that seems to echo off the surface of the water.

He counts automatically, assesses the distance to land. Another throb of light. The coast still a thin wood-coloured line.

The wind picks up, cold air moving in front of the storm.

And then there is a basal roll. The sound of a great weight landing. A slow tearing in the sky.

One repeated word now. No, no, no.

When it hits him there is a bright white light.

• • •

He swings the fish from the water, a wild stripe flicking and flashing into the boat, and grabs the line, twisting the hook out, holding the fish down in the footrests. It gasps, thrashes. Drums. Something rapid and primal, ceremonial, in the shallow of the open boat.

Flecks of blood and scales loosen, as if turning to rainbows in his hands as he picks up the fish and breaks its neck, feels the minute rim of teeth inside its jaw on the pad of his forefinger, puts his thumb behind the head and snaps.

The jaw splits and the gills splay, like an opening flower.

He was sure he would catch fish. He left just a simple note, 'Pick salad x'.

He looks briefly towards the inland cliffs, hoping the peregrine might be there, scanning as he patiently undoes the knot of traces, pares the feathers away from each other until they are free and feeds them out. The boat is flecked. Glittered. A heat come to the morning now, convincing and thick.

The kayak lilts. Weed floats. He thinks of her hair in water. The same darkened blonde colour.

It's unusual to catch only one. Or it was just a straggler. The edge of the shoal.

He retrieves a carrier bag from the drybag in back and puts the fish safe, the metal of it dulling immediately to cloth in his hands. Then he bails out the blood-rusted water that has come into the boat.

Fish don't have eyelids, remember. In this bright water, it's likely they are deeper out.

He's been hearing his father's voice for the last few weeks now.

I've got this one, though. That's enough. That's lunch anyway.

The bay lay just a little way north. It was a short paddle from the flat beach inland of him, with the caravans on the low fields above, but it felt private.

His father long ago had told him that they were the only ones that knew about the bay and that was a good thing between them to believe.

You'll set the pan on a small fire and cook the mackerel as you used to do together, in the pats of butter you took from the roadside cafe. The butter will be liquid by now, and you will have to squeeze it from the wrapper like an ointment.

He smiled at catching the fish. That part of the day safe.

I should bring her here. All these years and I haven't. It's different now. I should bring her.

The bones in the cooling pan, fingers sticky with the toffee of burnt butter.

He was not a talker. But he couldn't imagine sitting in the bay and not talking to his father.

There was a strange gurgle, a razorbill appeared, shuddered off the water, flicked its head and preened. It looked at him, head cocked, turned, looked over its shoulder as it paddled off a few yards. Then it dived again, was gone.

He took the plastic container from the front stow. It had warmed in the morning sun, and it seemed wrong and strange to him that it was warm. It was as if the ashes still had heat.

He unscrewed the lid partially, caught out by a sudden fear. That he would release some djinn, a ghost, the fatal germ. No. They're sterile. He threw science at the fear.

He'd had to go through so many possessions, things that exploded smally with memories over the last few weeks; but it was the opposite with the ashes. He was trying to hold away the fact that they knew nothing of what they were.

He knew their value was that they brought him out here. Something he had not done for a very long time. He found himself wanting to remind the ashes of events, things. He had to make them the physical thing of his father.

After the brief doubt he relaxed again. He could feel the current arc him out, its subtle shift away from shore. A strong draw to the seemingly still water.

He had a sense, out here, of peace. He could feel not only the proximity of the bay but a proximity to himself. He thought: Why do we stop doing the things we enjoy and the things we know are good for us?

When he had fetched the kayak out from under the tarp, there had been cobwebs, and earwigs were in amongst the hatchstraps.

It's not such a bad day.

He had not told her he was going. He'd expected it to be a weight he wanted to lift by himself.

There was a piping of oystercatchers, a clap of water as a fish jumped. He saw it for a moment, a silver nail. A thing deliberately, for a brief astounding moment, broken from its element.

He fades the kayak, lets it drift round the promontory, wiggling his ankles, working his feet loose with arrival. The water beneath him suddenly aglut. Sentinel somehow, with jellyfish. He wonders if they are a sign, of some increasing heat perhaps; but just as he feels a sense of settlement, the sound of music hits him.

A child knee high in the water, slapping at the waves. Another coming tentatively down the stones. A mother changing inside a towel.

The ashes sit perfectly in the drinks holder by his legs.

Laid out further off, a girl, at adolescent distance. The sound of her radio travelling. A pile of bright things.

The kayak jumps a little over the brief waves bouncing round the point, the sea seeming to goosebump for a moment, as if cold air goes across it. A kick under his hand, the ocean of her stomach.

The child has found a whip of kelp and slaps at the waves.

It's okay, Dad, he says. We'll come back later.

The sound of a jet ski, from the beach in front of the caravans. An urban, invasive sound.

We'll come back when they've gone.

Out in the distance, a small cloud. A white flurry. A crowd of diving birds.

They won't be here all day.

Then he paddles, the ashes by his legs, in a straight line out to sea.

*

Discover a NEW and convenient way to borrow your books

Search and reserve from our entire collection

Use your camera to issue your books

View your loans, reservations and payments

And much more.

Download it FREE on

 App Store ▶ Google Play

3 simple steps!

1 - Download each app onto your device.

2 - Select Hampshire Libraries

3 - Enter your borrower number and 4 digit pin.

Your Borrower Number:

Borrow eBooks and eAudiobooks online or with our library app.

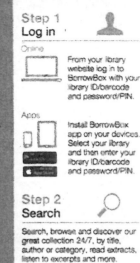

Step 1
Log in

Online

From your library website log in to BorrowBox with your library ID/barcode and password/PIN.

Apps

Install BorrowBox app on your devices. Select your library and then enter your library ID/barcode and password/PIN.

Step 2
Search

Search, browse and discover our great collection 24/7, by title, author or category, read extracts, listen to excerpts and more.

Step 3
Borrow ✓

Confirm your choice or reserve a title for later.

Step 4
Download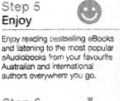

Download the complete eBook or eAudiobook instantly. When reserved titles are ready to download we'll email you.

Step 5
Enjoy 😊

Enjoy reading bestselling eBooks and listening to the most popular eAudiobooks from your favourite Australian and international authors everywhere you go.

Step 6
Revisit +

We're always adding new titles, so visit often and make the most of your library membership.

Borrow Box.

Designed and powered by Bolinda digital

Hampshire Libraries

YOUR LIBRARY

He wakes floating on his back, caught on a cleat by the elastic toggle of his wetsuit shoe. Around him hailstones melt and sink. They are scattered on the kayak, roll off as it bobs on the slight waves. There is a hissing sound. The hailstones melting in the water.

He stares around, shell-shocked, trying to understand, a layer of ash on the surface of the water. He cannot move his arms. They are held out before him as if beseeching the sky.

Dead fish lie around him in the water.

He gets himself to the boat, the boat to him, drawing it with his leg, shaking until he frees the lace, turns, kicks, twists, trying to lever with his useless arms. Somehow tips himself into the boat. A primal instinct to make land.

Live, he's thinking. *Live*.

A loud bell sounding in his head. The shock of an alarm.

His fishing rod on fire upon the water as he slips off the world again, and passes out.

19

His mouth is crusted with salt. He does not know where he is. There is a pyroclast of fine dried ash across his skin.

When he comes to, the strongest thing he feels is the tingling in his hands. It feels as if they are distant things, strange ringing bells. Finds out anew he cannot move his arms. He does not remember getting back into the kayak. Does not understand. The ground is moving. Is sure that if he moves he will abolish himself. Holds on to himself like a thought coming out of sleep.

He moves because he coughs, a cough made of glass. Slowly lifts himself. One eye closed with salt. Does not know why, why it will not open. His face has been in the floor of the kayak and the salt is from the evaporated water. The sun had come out hard after the storm and had evaporated the water, leaving the salt. It is in a crust on his eye. When he opens the other, the light blinds him.

It hurt to breathe because his whole body hurt. As if he had suffered a massive fall.

He blinked and struggled to raise himself a little more, the kayak shifting below him. The world slipping, rocking.

He felt the briefest flicker in his right arm, a wave of something and it spasmed, smashed unfeelingly against the inside of the boat and went dead again, fell now against his side, a fish flicking after suffocating. The other arm still stood out in front of him as if waiting to receive something. The tingling remained, like the pain when you crack your knee.

There was a ringing in his ears, a high insecty whine. He felt drunk. His head pumped full with something. He let the light in bit by bit, as if sipping it with his eye, raised his head and saw the water. For a moment he thought he was in some way blind; but then he understood: there was just the water, there was nothing else to see.

He processed the fact. Felt the languid rocking of the boat. For a while he stared at his knuckle. It had split and opened on the boat and bled thickly through his hand, but he could not feel it.

His legs seemed strong. They seemed strong in a way that made him think they were not part of his body. Like they were tools he had. He got them against the end of the cockpit and pushed himself up. Then sat, as if after being stunned.

The heat from the sun hit his face and he tried to move his head away, as if it were a bee worrying him. Then he closed his eye again. It was worse, the rocking and slipping under him. He felt sick with his eye closed.

He let it open, adjust again to the light. The light was coming down from the sky and up off the water so there was no place without light to look. After a while his eye accepted it.

The whine in his ears was predominant and the sea sound came to him as if from a shell.

He tried to open his mouth, suddenly aware of thirst.

What happened? What happened? His conscious-
ness a snapped cord his mind was trying to pull
back together.

He looks down at his left hand, a strange sense that
looking at it will bring it back, will help him move
it. It is fractalled with a strange blue pattern, seems
tattooed, a pattern the way ice forms on aeroplane
glass.

He does not understand.

Feels he must have been in some great crash.

His right arm comes back to him with the pain of releasing a trapped finger.

For a while it is wayward. Moveable, but numb, clumsy. He watches his hand as if it's a machine. Practises operating it, gripping, releasing, gripping. At first it is just an action, but gradually he registers the pressure of his grip. The tingling stays, but he has movement. The feel of it is like the sound that comes through the whining in his ears. Something acknowledged. A view through thick white glass.

He does not know how long he has been like this. Who he is. It could be moments. Days.

He sees a rouge burn through the dry salt on the muscle of his forearm, sees the line of his shinbone startled and red. Feels his face. Like something felt through packaging with his hand as it is. He hears more than properly feels the paper of his dry cracked lips. He has the strange conviction that if he opens his other eye he will see what happened.

As he tries again it's as if the eye leaves his face and flutters by him. A butterfly.

It takes him a while to focus, to believe it. Has forgotten there is other life. It puppets around him.

He cannot believe that a thing so small, breakable, is out here. A thing that cannot put down on the water. How far must we be from land? The butterfly settles on the bright lettering of the boat. He watches it open and close its wings in the sun. Opens and closes his good hand.

I might make the difference. I might be, out here, the freak thing that saves it. (Does he believe in purpose? He cannot remember. It feels now that he does.) It has to stay with me. I have to get it back.

He reaches up and scrapes the salt from his closed lid, picks at the hard crystal. He wets his hand in the water, blinks with the sting as he bathes his eye.

When he refocuses, the butterfly is gone. For a split second he believes again it was his eye, then he spots it, heading out over the water. As if something leaves him.

He felt a confusion, a kind of throb in his head. There was a complete horizon. A horizon *everywhere* around and no point of it seemed closer than another. It brought claustrophobia. He did not know if he was moving – if he was travelling. He could not tell in which direction if he was.

He felt only the rock, the sway, the dip and wallow of the boat.

———

The thump of the fin stirs him.

His head rested on the gunwale of the boat and the dark fin struck the boat inches from him.

He does not move. Cannot move. A few yards off the fin rises again, a half-metre sail out of the water, a gun-grey body.

It makes for the boat. He is frozen, still cannot move. His primal systems fire a wave of fear through him. He feels the adrenalin trying to get through him like water poured on ice, and the fin folds, disappears.

He is frozen, urinates, cannot move his head.

When it bumps the boat again it is as if the fin has grown tactile. It folds and flops, reaches over the gunwale of the boat; it is hallucinatory, cartoonish, like a sea lion's flipper; and then the body of the fish, clown-like, lolls side-on in the water, a disc the size of a table. They are eye to eye.

This cannot be happening, he thinks. The sunfish regards him, its curious fin folding, flopping. A strange ripple to the water in the otherwise lambent calm. This is it, he thinks. *This is it.*

The sunfish stayed with him for hours. It could be said it steered him. It was almost the size of the kayak in length and bumped and rubbed the boat with a droll instinct, as a cow might a post.

The sunfish is not fishable, not edible, and no instinct has been driven into it to stay away from man. And perhaps it was the warmth of the boat it liked, with the plastic heated in the sun. Or perhaps it was something more.

But it stayed and bumped the boat for hours and by doing so steered it; and it cannot be known whether it was deliberate, benevolent, that it did not steer the kayak further out to sea.

He woke to the sound, far off, of a speedboat engine. There was land in sight, like a presence that had woken him. For a moment he thought the warm sun on his neck was someone's breath.

His good arm had gone into the water and it was only when he lifted it he felt the sting where the little finger had been stripped.

It was torn and frayed to the first knuckle, skinned through to the flesh and swollen and ragged with water. The pain was searing and hot. The nail was still there but had tooth marks where the little fish had bitten at it. When he touched the finger, his head spun.

In the centre of the kayak, before him, was a locker and he had some sureness there was a first-aid kit there. Given what he did not know, he felt confused at the sureness. He tried the screw of the locker but it would not give. Saw, on his skin, a grey dust above the point his arm had lain in the water, felt the knowledge of it flutter, float inside him. A sense of himself, a fly trapped the wrong side of glass.

When he tried the locker again, the pain of his finger shot round his body. He gave up. Somehow he knew it was always stubborn. Just accept the pain. Focus on the fact the land is there.

He knew now he had gone out for something, and he knew this was his boat. But it was only now he truly recognised the paddle was gone and understood it. He was less spacey, and more functional. With that came a low panic.

The idea of breath on his neck lay under everything. A suspicion someone had been left behind.

He turned in his seat and reached for the drybag, husbanding the finger. Used his teeth and hand to open it, spilled out the looser things, took the sunblock, the T-shirt, the old cloth.

When he saw the address label on the bag he saw his name. It was like looking into an empty cup. Then he heard a voice say it. The knowledge it gave down was as delicate as an image sitting on the surface of the water, disrupting as he moved to reach it.

He let it go, instinctively.

It does not matter who you are. You know what you are physically, and that you're in a kayak in the middle of the ocean. It only matters what you are, right now.

His face hurt to touch. His skin was parched and sore and was stretched and gritty with salt.

He rubbed the sunblock in. A baffling thought of holidays. Worked urgently, as if the next few moments were vital.

His ears were blistered and cracked, he rubbed the lotion into his hair. He did his dead hand and was frightened by it. That he could not feel it. That the arm lay so inert. It had stretched out now, dormant. He had a sort of horror at his body. How long has this taken to happen? How long have I been out here?

He looked again at his useless hand, the now purplish fern-like pattern. It seemed to follow his veins, mark tiny capillaries, a leaf skeleton disappearing under the tide-line of ash into the sleeve of his top.

He felt the arm for breaks. Any misangle, like a cracked stick. Nothing. Believed then, horribly, that it was blood poisoning.

A wave of sick went through him.

He knew he had gone out on the kayak. Remembered loading it onto the car, gulls along the shallow river, luminous somehow in the early morning light, then drifting out at sea. The time in between was gone. Like a cigarette burn in a map.

With what he had to hand, he had to choose what part of him got burned.

He took the T-shirt and wet it, wrapped it on his head, the touch of it a heat at first against his burnt skin. But then it cooled, there was a sort of weight lifted, as if the sun stopped pressing.

Tucking them into his shorts, he laid the spare carrier bags as best he could over his knees, looked at the land, just an inch or so high on the far-off horizon. He had a total conviction that things would be okay. Heard a voice he trusted tell him; wondered if it was just his own voice, that he could not recognise.

He unzipped the pocket of his buoyancy aid and fumbled out the phone, dropped it into his lap as he popped open the waterproof pouch. He turned it upside down and tipped the phone out, thunk on the boat, picked it up and tried to start it. Nothing.

Take it apart. Let it dry out.

He struggled with it until the back slipped off. There against the battery lay the wren feather.

He trapped it with his thumb. Held it carefully. His memory like a dropped pack of cards.

Next door's cat. Its strange possessive mewling, crouched over the wren, the bird like a knot of wood.

The bird vibrated briefly when he picked it up, a shudder of life. Then flew away.

He could not picture her, but the sense of her came back.

They had kept a feather each.

The idea of her, whoever she might be, seemed to grow into a point on the horizon he could aim for. He believed he would know more as he neared her.

He put the feather and the pieces of the phone together into the drybag, then fitted the phone pouch over his fingers, leaving his forefinger and thumb free. He felt sick as the little finger touched the plastic but he was determined, and the pain, in a way, was a little coach to him. He braced himself because he knew it would be worse when he began. Then he leaned to the water and paddled.

The pain was like a trigger.

When he passed out, it was like another white light shot through him.

The storm had begun miles out. A patch of air eventually succumbed to tiny variances until it became unstable. Under different pressures, cloud built up and travelled, pushing cool air on in front.

As it went, the cloud itself began to polarise. The positive and negative forces in it segregated. Negativity built up in the base sending step leaders out – negative energy, reaching down in lines – until the ground responded with positive streamers, feelers waiting patiently.

When the two met, current flowed between them, trying to neutralise the separation that had occurred in the cloud. To short circuit it.

The lightning is not the strike. It is the local effect of the strike. The air around it explodes.

Shouts. Faintly. Loud shouts that reach him quieter than whispers. That seem to carry on the air like faintly visible things. The ringing in his head is a hum now, a low choir, the flick of water on the boat constant, random, like the sound of work in the distance.

He senses movement, just a shifting air, the smallest breeze that bears the shouts; a sure current, the kayak drifts. Goes sideways past the shingle bay.

He is in a dream. He sees, there, a penguin crowd of people bathing in their clothes. In black-and-white suits. They are playing in the water. Children in waistcoats. As if a wedding has run into the sea.

Where am I?

He lifts his arm. They are far off. Tiny on the shore. Tries to shout. Shouts like a puncture. Like a hiss of air.

Hears the draw and swash of the waves breaking in the bay, sees the children jump the water. The sound of play. A bus parked on the road behind the beach.

Are they celebrating the end of the world? he thinks.

I am dreaming. They are bathing in their clothes.

The boy had been given the binoculars for his birthday which was at the start of the holiday and they had hardly left his neck since then. As well as looking through them, he loved the rubbery smell of them.

He was so attached to the binoculars that he did not even go into the water.

As a baby he had liked to stretch his hands out at an object until it was brought to him, and it was a sort of magic to him, how the binoculars seemed to do just that. To bring things up.

The other children were bored of trying to splash him and his parents had given up trying to persuade him to put the binoculars away for a while and go and play; and he stood on the beach near the water with his eyes stuck to the lenses, as if there was something wrong with him.

He was the only one who noticed the distant kayak, a small splinter out to sea, a pale speck on which sat a lone man, his head bound, it seemed to the boy, like some strange Arab.

He watches the land fade, as if it slowly sinks into the ocean.

There is the humming in his ears and the constant sound of breeze now, like a wind through trees. An illusion that the breaking tide is close.

The sun, and there is nothing he can do about it, is on the way down. He feels the temperature dropping, a respite of its physical pressure. It is still hot, beating, but with the slight relief there is a slow, sickening certainty.

He has bailed out the cockpit best he can. The cloud of dark piss, the salt rimes, the tide mark of salt that shows how the water has evaporated.

Scales of mackerel decal the inside, here and there a zip of dried blood. The texture of the plastic, bumped, like a dashboard, for some reason makes him think of being in a car. He wets his face with the damp cloth, now and then.

If you can see people fully dressed, you might see anything. How will you know, if she comes back to mind, that she is real? That you have not just conjured her?

He undoes the phone again, fishes out the wren feather and holds it.

He feared the state of him was frightening. That if he just stayed still, his memory would approach.

You'll know. You'll surely know.

For a while, as he drifts, it is not the thirst, nor the sun, nor the open space around him that occupies him most. It is the need to stand up.

Still, his memory is out of reach, things approaching, dipping, disappearing. A butterfly, nearly knowledge. He thinks of the state of his skin, does not know if he had started out clean shaven, knows, though, that his stubble grows at uneven rates.

He tries the locker again. Pressures and turns with his thumb and finger, patiently until the screw hatch jumps and, after a few hard-fought-for millimetres, rattles loose.

He fishes out the built-in pouch, squeezes the toggle and loosens the drawstring. Feels, for a horrible moment, that he has opened some plug.

He unrolls the first-aid bag, the rip of Velcro a strange abrupt noise that seems to tear the fabric of sounds he has got used to. With the violence of the act, some of the dried ash falls flaked from his skin, as if drawing attention to itself.

He opens his dry mouth best he can – winces at the chapped cracks of his lips – and bites down on a roll of gauze, uses an antiseptic towel on his finger. He even smells the sting, as he did as a child, Dettol on a grazed knee. He rocks it away, humming through the gauze, rocks until he can open his eyes on the pain.

He tears the dressing packet, puts the pad down on his thigh, and puts it clumsily round his finger. Then he starts the papery tape with his teeth and gets an end around the dressing, jamming the tape-roll in his knees, makes a clumsy bandage. Fits on a plastic finger guard. The effort makes him reel.

The water slapping the side of the boat picks up intentfully. It's just the angles, he tells himself. It's because I'm changing the weight.

He leans over the front stow, unclips it and draws out the large drybag, sees the small pan in the hold, the rolled cloth that holds cutlery, a wooden spoon.

He feels odd little humpback lurches to the water, an empty sickness without food. Has a bizarre sense that he could reach out and put his hand on her stomach.

He reaches out a carrier bag. It is heavy with a bottle of water and a bottle of dark beer. He stares at the beer for a moment. He was going somewhere. He was going to drink a beer. Her stomach. Then, fumbling, urgent, he takes a drink of water, warm, hot almost, wets his mouth, lips, lets it pour wastefully over his chin. There is a shock to the immediacy of its effect, a voice screaming: do not waste this; do not drink too much. He brings the bottle down, a sort of fear to him. Dab at it, he told himself. Don't drink too fast. Thinks of watering a dry plant too quickly.

You have to save this, he thinks. Dry dirt will repel the thing it needs the most. Stares again for a moment at the beer.

Empties out the dry bag:

Small gas stove. Espresso cup. Coffee maker. Small plastic box of coffee. Tackle box with traces, hooks, weights, swivels, lures. Thick jumper. Reel of fishing line. Cagoule.

You went out. You went out too far fishing.

He keeps out the thick jumper. Tucks the cagoule in by the seat. Does a brief inventory of the boat.

One litre water, less that gone. A bottle of dark beer. Two dry bags, large and small. Tackle box. Small gas stove. T-shirt. Fishing line. Espresso cup. Knife and fork. Sunblock. Coffee maker. Car keys. Wooden spoon. Frying pan. Small plastic box of coffee. Thick jumper. Old cloth. Small towel. Drink bottle. Cagoule. First-aid kit containing: dressings; plasters; emergency blanket; surgical tape; antiseptic wipes; needle and thread; roll of gauze; finger guards; painkillers.

He does not add: one man. One out of two arms. Four out of ten fingers. No paddle. No torch. One dead phone.

The sun drops beautifully.

He takes off the buoyancy aid and pulls on the thick jumper, useless arm first. The smell of the jumper triggers something, but it is like a piano key hitting strings that are gone.

He puts the cagoule on, again the useless arm first, but cannot zip it up. Then he puts back on the buoyancy aid, in the doing of it, loses the T-shirt from his head. Watches, stoical, as it floats out on the water like a strange fish. There is a slight swell to the sea now, and the pan and bottle in the forward hold roll and scrape inside, roll and scrape with the loll of the boat.

He scoots forward again, opens the hold cover, horribly aware in that instant how small the kayak is, stuffs the pan and bottle under the drybag to jam them.

Of all the things to put up with, that would be too much. The persistent clunking. It was one of the few things he had any say in.

He has a horrible fear of falling out of the boat. Its frail platform. Of being afloat in the coming darkness. Suddenly can't help the sense that there are cities under the sea.

He rearranges the bungee at the back bay, nearly vomits as he upsets the balance enough to think he's going in, and slips it over himself like a seatbelt. He fastens one end of the paddle leash to the carry handle, the other round his ankle. It is nothing. But it is all that he can do.

You took it off. The paddle leash. It kept catching the cleat as you paddled out. There were gannets folding into the water around you.

Into the smaller drybag he puts the things he thinks he needs the most.

Bottle of water. Now empty drink bottle. Sunblock. Knife. Fishing reel. The mackerel wrapped up in a bag. Emergency blanket. Dead phone. Keys. For some reason he cannot discard the phone, the keys.

Then he clips the drybag round one of the straps on his buoyancy aid.

With dark the cold hits. It is immediate, comes with a sureness that it will get colder.

For a long time he fights the need to piss. Or what feels like a long time.

He lifts off the bungee, kneels in the boat, and pisses off the side, a weak stream, a stench he hears pattering on the side of the gunwale, feels it mist his bare legs. But where it hits the water there is a sudden light, a gorgeous phosphorescence.

When he's done, careful of his hurt finger, he puts his hand partially in the water, waves it, disturbs, sees its shape green and fluid like a separate creature. He feels a sense of wonder. A wondrous sense of what has happened to him. The impossibility of it all. Begins to feel hungry.

When he sits back he redoes the bungee round himself. For a long while holds the image of his hand.

He looks at the stars, sees those on the horizon. That some of them might be the lights of ships, of land, he can't allow himself to think. Cannot allow himself to imagine the warmth, the food, the safety they would mean. It is better they are stars. That they are out there somewhere in the same infinity as him. That they are not real beacons.

The swell has picked up. The boat dips, sways as if two unseen hands shift it, as if panning for rare minerals. With his empty stomach, he feels a constant bowl of nausea.

He has no measurement of time. *Time* seems too specific a word to him. He thinks of whiles, moments – things less measurable. And for a long while he watches the stars, the thin double halo girding the moon, rocking to and fro, building his own constellations, finding his own patterns, drawing his own imaginary lines.

How long? How long has it been? Is this my first night out? I would have been thirstier, wouldn't I, if I'd been out longer?

He looks. Looks. A child awake in a dark bedroom. And, after a while, the stars seem to fade, at first very slowly. He does not know if it's illusion, but they start to go out, like houselights across a night landscape.

He focuses on one high above until it dims, his eye still as the boat sways. There is a definite chop come to the sea. He knows it, with a passive horror.

He unwraps the emergency blanket, the silver foil of it speaking with reflected light. He lays it to one side beneath him, shifts onto it and pulls the sheet across him, tucks it round again, just his one good arm free.

His feet are cold; the air, he can even feel, is cold. Settling like a sheet. But there is the dissipating heat out of his raw skin.

The boat shifts up and down, a lullaby hush.

One by one, the stars go out.

*

It is not from real sleep the noise brings him, but from a strange shallow place. The sleep we have when we travel. It is cold and it is pitch black. Blacker when he opens his eyes, blacker than it was when they were closed – a stunning nothingness. He is hardly conscious. And he hears the child's voice. Hears the clear troubling cry of a child.

This is not real, he thinks.

He feels that his heart is slow, his breathing flaccid.

There is the cry again.

The cold a complete tiredness. A calm. Like an acceptance of drowning.

I can go now, he thinks. I've done my best. He feels passive towards it. He is so cold that if there was any challenge to him he would gently yield, let it happen.

Cold now, he thinks. It's okay. A thought of holding someone's hand. It's okay now. Slip. Away.

The football rattle of a magpie by the boat. The sound of splashes in the dark. A kind of kazoo sound.

A spray of water covers him, pattering the plastic blanket, falls on him warmer than his skin and he opens his eyes, sees the green light, the perfect shape of dolphins playing round the boat.

It is a spell. They are a quick shape, a liquid in their own right through the black water, bright spirits under him.

Somewhere he feels his ticking heart, an engine trying to start. Was he nearly gone? *Was* he gone? The child's cry, close by now, of the dolphin calf; and the mother breaks the water, a luminous green form leaving a figure of itself in the air, bright water dropping, a glow, crashing colour landing...back... into the water.

The calf sounded so human. A baby in an upstairs room.

Stay alive, he thinks.

A bright tail, beautiful triangle.

You have to stay alive.

PART II

He woke with a strange specific clarity. Dawn had come with no chorus of sound. A stiffness had set into his body. The boat seesawed gently. The water had stilled again in the night.

He lay there letting his body warm up.

The night he had come through seemed tangible, as if it hung around him. It had passed, and it had left him alive, and with three solid simple things: her, the child, his physical ability. These, now, were landmarks.

He sat up. His skin where it was bare had tightened. Where he touched there was a fine sand of dried salt.

He felt the kayak buoy on the meniscus of the water, had a clear image: prawns gathering with the bold-ness of small birds around her bare feet in a pool.

He spots it, absolutely motionless in the still water, riding the faint change in the surface as he nears.

It is a doll, floating. He feels as if he has found a lost child. As if he squeezes her shoulder, reassuringly, you will be safe, when he picks it from the water.

Under the starfish colour of her dress her body is filled with polystyrene peas; they show through the wet-loosened wool.

Her eyes are a deep blue. He feels he will damage her if he wrings the water from her, cannot bring himself to do it.

He undid the buoyancy aid and got out of it, unclipping the drybag from it and placing them before him. Strangely, taking off the buoyancy aid was like taking off a rucksack or some thing he had carried on a walk.

He took off the cagoule and rolled it, stuffed it in by his seat, everything with one hand. Then he got himself out from the seatbelt he had made.

He was uncertain of it, but he seemed to sense more from his deadened arm. Still the electric bell rang in it. But it was as if he had the idea of it at least, that it was not just a dead foreign weight.

He stretched himself best he could, bent his legs, pumped his ankles. In the doing of it, his lips split and bled. He saw beneath him a flock of jellyfish, like negligees. Felt they were a sign. Some augury. An echo. That he had seen this before.

With the knowledge of her had come the need to ease her worry. It was impossible for him to believe he would die, but it was possible for him to believe he could leave her alone. Her and the child.

The real fear he was trying to keep the lid on was for them.

He took the fish from the carrier bag in the drybag and the fishing knife and put the fish down on the side of the boat.

It's raw fish. People pay for that. There was a hollow gawp in his stomach.

He cut down behind the gills, turned the blade flat and drew it along, feeling it bump over the bones of the spine. The fillet peeled off like a flap, the meat changed and cured in the heat. It looked like weathered translucent plastic. It moved like the thick skin on a blister.

He ate the fillet and chewed it, the salt meat of it, but spat out the skin which he could not break down. It left a taste of oil, a metally feeling on the roof of his mouth. Then he drank some water. It had cooled again in the night.

You could cut the top off, invert it in the neck. A memory of a stream, strange-armoured caddisfly larvae, small fish darting in the bottle. No, you'd catch nothing bigger than your thumb. And you'd have nothing to drink from. You can't sacrifice the bottle.

Even if you had a pen, and some paper, to send some note, trust the tide to take it home, you cannot sacrifice the bottle.

This is going to be about rhythm. You cannot control anything else, remember. But you can control your rhythm. You have half a small fish and four inches of water. If you grow impatient it will go wrong.

The thick heat seemed to have lifted. The sun came but there were sparse white clouds, a clarity in the air.

The foily taste of the fish grew as he swallowed the water, brought a strange sting to his mouth.

You have to conserve energy; and you have to be patient.

When he turned round to stow the drybag, he saw
the land.

This is just rhythm, he said. You cannot race. You will move the boat only a little, but you must not be impatient.

He tied a trace onto the line, knotting it awkwardly with his one hand to the swivel he held in his mouth. He clipped a lead weight to the end of the trace. Could smell the sunblock on his hand.

You will move only a little and you must not race. Just proceed. That's all it is about. When you are tired, rest; but do not let the boat turn around and undo the work.

He hung the trace in the water, the colourful feathers immediately shivering like small fish, then let the line play out from the reel.

When it was some metres out he wound the line around the carry handle of the boat and dropped the reel into the cockpit.

He took off the jumper and folded it into a pad. Then he knelt up on it, put on the buoyancy aid, and picked up the small frying pan.

After a few strokes he got the boat around.

The pain of resting on his burning shins balanced the pain of using his raw finger into a tough hold-able thing.

That's the land, he said. That's everything.

It was a low undulating line on the horizon.

It is all about rhythm now.

And he began to paddle.

It does not matter where you land. You can make fire. All you would need would be the empty bottle, a little water.

He imagined the bright dot suddenly blinding, a halo of ash and the sudden scent of burning, seaweed firing with a quick crack.

Find a cove. Get yourself to a cove with fresh water, and you will survive. You can eat limpets if you have to.

If you disappear you will grow into a myth for them. You will exist only as absence. If you get back, you will exist as a legend.

He fell into the rhythm of paddling three times each side. Long slow strokes that were an attempt to drag the boat, as if he were pulling it along a rope.

He took his bigger breaths as he changed sides, his stomach muscles burning immediately, a sort of dumb ache happening straight away in his hand. Even the missing extra leverage of his little finger made it more awkward.

When he missed the water he fell forward, having no other arm to catch himself.

Just adjust, he said. It is not easy. Just adjust to it. The call was to do something rather than nothing. It's a new movement. Your body will get used to it.

The fish took the line while he was resting. It did not seem the land was any closer.

You know the boat is moving though. It has to be, he said quietly within himself.

Every so often as he paddled he would look over his shoulder at the short reassuring wake. The wake that shows the calm water.

It is moving. It is.

He sat to give relief to his knees and was glad when the nose of the boat did not go round, that it seemed the kayak accepted the direction he had put it in. He thought of it for a while like a cooperative horse.

The fish hit and with the transfer of struggle the boat seemed to tense and squeeze and flutter. He hauled in the line, having to trap it with his knee against the gunwale as he drew it.

He saw the blue edge of the golden fish as he got the trace to the surface. It was foul-hooked through the fin. Not a fish he had seen before.

He had caught it on a deep line and as he lifted it clear of the surface it glimmered and flashed and seemed to leap. Then it came loose of the hook and fell back, disappeared into the water.

It did not seem to belong. He had the idea, in the grey waters that he knew, that the fish were grey. Or silver and green: the colours of the water. It was a shock to him to see the gold red and the bright blue of the fish, as if it was from somewhere warm.

He thought again of the huge table-shaped fish and did not know if it was truly real.

Am I in different water? he thought. Have I drifted somewhere? He was sure he sensed towns and villages beneath him, sunken. How in the bay at home they believe you could still hear the bell ringing in the drowned tower from an ancient town. How his grandfather as a child saw a U-boat rise by the spit before the village.

He thought of the strange sunfish. The heat. Was that just yesterday? Time was a wide ocean. He'd lost the occasion of things as he floated and remembering the sunfish was like remembering a dream.

In the fluttering that had come to the boat and through the line he remembered the wren vibrating briefly in his hand. The signs of life under her surface.

He looked up at the land. On the other horizon, a dark line of cloud was appearing, like a shelf.

He unwrapped the mackerel from the carrier bag and cut off the head.

Trapping it then against the side of the boat with his knee, he ran a large hook through the mouth and out through the flesh and back so it came through the nose.

He clipped the line that was attached to the hook to the feather trace and moved the weight so it was linked from the baited hook. Then he threw out the rig and let out the line.

As the grey weight dropped he imagined the sunk U-boat sounding out of control through the deep water, the horror of the crew entombed. No understanding of what has truly happened to them; a horrible iron chrysalis careening like a sinking weight into the tower, the slow animation of the drowned structure, shattering, the great bell, loosed, thumping into the bed of the ocean

…the weight bounce and settle on the seabed, the accuracy go from the line. How long it takes the weight to land. A grey falcon folding through the sky, a thunk of mass.

When she realises I am missing she will look on the cliffs, thinking I will be there. I should have told her I was coming out. Why? Why would I have not?

He imagined what it must have been like, in that first moment when they realised the dyke was breached. The flat rich land asheet suddenly with salt water. What if they had survived, continued to live there below the water. What would they think of the submarine, then?

The abstract thought seemed to give him hope. That he could think of something beyond himself.

Stay aware, he thought. You are not beaten.

By now the heat came thickly again. A different sense to the air, but no escape from the sun.

He took the cagoule and cut away the hood from it, put the hood awkwardly on his head.

Again he paddled.

If you couldn't see land you could drift. But there is land, so you have to do this. This is going to be about rhythm, remember that.

And suddenly and gently he recognised his father's voice.

You cannot get angry.

It made him very still for a while, made him stop.

If you get angry, it is better to be still and do nothing.

He understood, with quiet wondrous horror, the foundation of ash still in places on him.

Slowly let the voice sink in.

What of you, if you do not get back? What will you sound like in the mind of your child?

He pushed the thought away.

You cannot get angry that your effort is not moving you faster. It will not make sense, in a flurry of anger or hope or ambition or anything that is not to do with rhythm, to try to race, because you will not be able to keep it up. You will get tired and distraught and you will give up. Keep rhythm. It is all about rhythm.

If you can just get close enough, then you'll be in the play of the tides. Then it will be about rhythm and luck. If you get the ingoing tide. That will be your landfall.

With every stroke he tried to stave off the cold leaking recognition: you are miles away. You are hardly progressing. There will be another night. And there is no more water to drink.

The last of it had seemed to evaporate. A tiny slug. He hardly felt it as he drank it.

I could get out, he thought. He had the idea of making a cord with the drawstring of the cagoule. Or the paddle leash.

I could get out and swim the kayak along. Rest on it when I get tired.

But then he thought of the reality of the water. The idea of it now was like being at a great height. It was a great drop below the frail platform of the boat.

He was trying to do maths. He was doing the maths as a rhythm as he paddled.

How long can a body go without water? Really? Not what we think. How long without food? How far off is the horizon?

Turn half your height in feet to miles. The horizon is that far off. If I'm three foot kneeling here, I can see one mile and a half. But the land is beyond that.

If it is three miles then the land is more. Say seven miles off. Be conservative. Which is about ten kilometres.

What am I doing? A metre per stroke? Some five metres for each side I paddle? With the momentum. Five. Say five, ten metres together, twenty metres a minute. With a break every three of four goes. A hundred metres every ten minutes.

He worked with numbers he could do.

Let's say half a kilometre an hour.

He looked up at the land. It just wasn't possible. Not by nightfall. And then the boat braked in the water. Suddenly. Veered, jerked, even against the forward pull of his paddle stroke.

He saw the line go taut from the carry handle, buzz with strain. The kayak shifted.

It's caught, he said. It's snagged. It's the drift of the water making it feel it's being pulled.

When he put down the frying pan he could hardly open his hand. Then the boat went inexorably through the water.

He grabbed the line, tried to lift it and it immediately cut into his palm. A quick sharp paper cut with a pain that seemed to have a noise to it. The line zipped in the water, cut out from the flank of the boat, oblique, then went slack.

He leant forward on his knees, tried to reach the little pad of cloth. There was a strike and the boat moved again, the nose turning this time into the line.

He took the line with the pad in his hand and heaved with all his might, felt a sheer force against him, a surging weight that turned the boat, seemed to haul it sideways for a time then faced it out to sea. They gathered speed.

When he cut the line the boat thumped with the release and for a moment hissed through the water. Then went quiet, and slack.

He looked down at his bleeding hand. Thick cloud on the horizon. The loose line riffling in the breeze.

A kind of quiet came inside him.

It was like a portent.

All of his life he's had a recurring dream: the car leaves the road. It is never the impact that terrifies him, wakes him. His fear comes the moment he feels the car go.

His life does not pass before his eyes. There is even a point he feels calm. But then he sees the faces of the people he loves. He sees their faces as they see him go.

He held the drybag against the gunwale and pushed the knife through from inside.

When he had the address label loose he carefully wrapped the drybag down past the bit he'd cut, and clipped it.

He looped the fishing line into a slipknot and secured the label against the doll. Then he wrapped it round and round, leaving the address visible, until he was sure it would stay on.

Because he could not write anything, he told everything he wanted to say to the doll. The few simple sentences.

When it came to it, he could not put her back into the water.

A revenant of a dream. An absence, or, he does not know, a memory, *tunt tunt*, warping, like sound carried on the breeze. Swash filtering in the pools.

I have slipped off the world, he thinks.

I see you stand, at the edge of the shore, watch a man get into the water. You think, for a moment, as the boat floats behind, he is bringing news of me.

You brush a strand of hair from your face and feel sick when he takes off his gloves to talk, sure now the news will come.

The lick came into the waves late afternoon and with it a wide swell to the water. The clouds now were an intentful dark strip on the horizon and they were incoming and the breeze came before them brushing the crests of the waves, bringing patches over the water like a cat's fur brushed the wrong way.

The handle of the frying pan was sticky from his bleeding hand. He had continued to paddle on and off. Had thrown up after eating the second piece of fish and that had affected him.

There was a thin bare moisture in the breeze and every now and then he opened his mouth to it. The small area of his body was acting as a sail and the boat had picked up speed. And gradually he neared the land. The colours now distinguishable.

It was less easy to bear, having the land in view. He did not think 'if I die you must find someone else'; he could not think that. He felt a massive responsibility.

He wanted to make sure she knew how to reset the pilot light on the boiler. Pictured a coffee cup, never moved, the little left liquid growing into a ghost of dust. The note, 'Pick salad x'.

Get to the land. That's all you need to do. They will find you. Or you could wait, until your arm is better, and get home.

Stay close to shore. There will be a harbour. Sooner or later.

Or get to a buoy. Get to a buoy and hang until they come to check the pots.

Don't think of the water, just the surface.

He runs his good hand over the pattern, his broken veins. The burst lace inside him. A force gone through him.

It does not matter how far it is. If you stayed close to the shore. Use the buoyancy aid, and kick. It would be like walking. Lie back, and kick into the water.

You have to just trust the float, he thinks. The chute will open. The rope will hold. It is a jump from space.

They will find you, if you stay close to the shore.

When he saw it he thought it was a bag or sack floating stiffly in the water. It was a fence banner. He
turned the boat frantically, the handle of the pan
rattling and worked loose now.

Seaweed and algae had grown on the banner so it
looked somehow furred, like a great dead animal on
the surface of the water.

He pushed at the fur of algae and it slid easily,
giving out a strange warm water, uncovered a bright
picture of a family car.

There were metal eyelets in the corners and along
the edge of the plasticked canvas, swollen and rusted
in the water, and as he lifted it into the boat the
banner caught and bridled in the breeze, the car
rippling.

The plane of the water surface had changed now
and as he scraped the bigger patches of algae from
the banner with the back of his knife the kayak
tilted forwards and ran, then stalled; then its back
sunk a little and it bobbed; then it happened again,
a slow hefting on the wave.

He doubled the fishing line and fed it slackly through an eyelet of the banner and brought it back, tying it to the cleat where he clipped his seat. He did the same at the other corner.

Then he cut the toggle away from one end and took the drawstring from the hem of the cagoule to give himself a cord. With that he tied the other corners of the banner around the carry handles of the boat.

When he put his feet to the banner and lifted it aloft, the wind caught it with a snap.

He had the idea of the land as a magnet. If he could get close, it would draw him in.

The light dropped prematurely with the rain. At first thin, persistent grey drizzle. Even after all his time at sea, the rain seemed to bring a fresh smell of damp salt.

He cut the top from the bottle and filled it where the rain ran down the sail of banner. His skin loosened. His eyes stung with salt that the rain washed into them. Every so often he bailed out the boat.

It was a light, saturating rain that pattered sharply on the cagoule he had put on. Through it the land was visible and grey. Very sparsely, lights appeared.

The wind now brushed the crests from the waves and it filled the sail, blew a light spray into the boat.

In the falling light it seemed that a shadow lifted up from the water, and something went past him. Bat-like, implications. A low whirr of shearwaters. A ghost.

He thought then, for the time he had been drifting, how he had not seen other birds. He had not seen a plane.

What if this is it? What if there has been some quiet apocalypse? Some sheet of lethal radiation I somehow survived. Some airborne plague.

He thought of the sunburn on his body, a momentary scald. Of the sunfish, the butterfly. A sect, drowning themselves in the water. The heat, liquid. Sluicing from the air.

Partly, there was relief in the idea. That he would not hurt them if they were already gone.

He shook the thought away.

The premature evening stars. How she stuck glow-in-the-dark dots to the ceiling of the nursery.

When it was beyond doubt that the land was nearing he had wept quietly. The tears had gone into his mouth.

He lifted the banner a little at the end of his feet and saw the growing details of the land. Then he rested, looked at the picture of the bright car. He could not get it from his mind that she would be waiting on the beach; the bell of her stomach.

It was only then he recognised the danger, staring at the car, the car leaves the road. I have no way to steer. The land now is a wall.

The light is going. The storm is coming.

He felt it in the water first. A kind of filling, like a muscle tensing.

The sea is getting up.

I'm better off further out. If I can stay in the boat. If I can stay on it. Ride the storm out.

The water would get harsher as he neared the land. The shallower water and the shore could kill him.

He could hear now, distantly, the boom of water hitting cliffs. A low echo. The first sound of land.

Hold out. All you need is daylight. You could go in on your own if you could see. Trust the buoyancy aid, trust the float. Just swim yourself in.

He turned, tried to look back out to sea. A dark wall sliding in.

You have to get away. Get out from the cliffs.

He leant frantically and tried to draw the kayak round, the scream of his finger a white noise. Helping him.

The sea seemed to swell. Tauten. Refuse. An intent coming to the surface. But it seemed impossible to go voluntarily into the water.

How can I stay out here? You cannot take the kayak into the run of the storm. You don't have a way to.

All this, waiting, and now.

He sensed the shore, like the cold air at the mouth
of a cave.

The squall came in like a landslide, with a physical force.

It cracked into the sail and drove the nose down and he struggled to keep the boat level, the cockpit filling and spewing.

As the sea picked up he knew it was useless. The sign sang and hissed and seemed to bolt from him. You feel the strike, he knew. You feel the strike coming.

He cut the cord, sending the banner out like a kite. A bird flapping after being struck. Then the line snapped and it ripped free, skimmed off over the water. A car out of control.

He held the carry handle, tried to jam his useless arm behind the seat.

You should have kept the banner. You should have kept it as a sea anchor. It might have kept you on to the waves.

His father was everywhere now, as if he had entered the sky.

There was no control. There was a randomness to the water. As if a great weight had been dropped into it. He was horrified, tried to persuade himself they could not see him, they were not watching.

The back tipped, tipped him, plunged with the whole body of the kayak shuddering.

In the half-light it was as if the boat had been driven into a dark rut.

He tried to press the kayak into the water, to cling on, as if to the flank of some great beast. Tried to lean the kayak into the waves. But the boat went round. The sea was up now. An uprushing ground.

He thought of the land, the rock. He was gone now beyond any sense of danger to a blank expectant place as he undid the paddle leash and the world seemed to go from underneath him.

I do not want the boat to come with me. It would be like a missile.

Trust the float now. You have to trust the float.

If a bird the size of a wren can survive in the jaws
of a cat.

He locked eyes with her. The doll was gone.

He knew he was going then. He knew.

Acknowledgements

Thanks to L.B. and all at Granta Books, and to Euan
and the team at Heath.

Thanks also to the shore crew. I won't go so far out
next time.

Author's Note

In the early stages of writing this book I looked into talismans held to keep a sailor safe at sea. I had written the wren feather in before this.

A wren feather, it turns out, was said to save a man from shipwreck.

Later I discovered Celts believed the wren to be the bearer of celestial fire. Its feathers gave protection against lightning.